# Every Llama Needs a Scarf

**Written by**
**Tunisia Williams**

**Illustrated by**
**Jessica Roberts**

Skylight Books

An imprint of Tandem Light Press
950 Herrington Rd.
Suite C128
Lawrenceville, GA 30044

Tandem Light Press hardcover edition 2021

ISBN: 987-1-7353210-5-9
Library of Congress Control Number: 2020932731

PRINTED IN THE UNITED STATES OF AMERICA

This book is
dedicated in memory
of our little angels,

**Nyah** and **Zion.**

# Acknowledgments

I give all honor to God. Thank you to my husband, Robert, for your love, patience, and support. Thank you to my friends and family.

A special thank you to Pastors Claude and Regina Harris and New Life Ministries for teaching me to put God first, pursue my dreams, and to "say something crazy."

I would also like to thank Dr. Pamela Larde and the Tandem Light Press staff for your patience, kindness, and support in making my dream a reality.

ZOO PARADE

Every
BEAR
needs a beret
to wear in
zoo parades.

Every
# OWL
## needs specs
to show
he is wise.

Every
PARROT
needs shades
to shield her big,
bright eyes.

# Every
# LION
## needs an umbrella
## for long walks in
## the rain.

# Every
# SLOTH
## needs a book
### to read while
### on the train.

# Every
# BOA
# needs a fedora
## to keep his
## noggin warm.

Every GECKO needs a baton to twirl while she performs.

Every MANATEE needs his tea to sip on right at noon.

# Every
# SHEEP
## needs to jump
## to hurdle over
## the moon.

# Every CAMEL

needs a duvet to warm his bed of hay.

# Every
# CRAB
## needs a bay
## to lounge on
## sunny days.

Every

# PANDA

needs a purse

for lip gloss

and perfume.

And every
MOUSE
needs a mink,
though she shouldn't
wear it in June.

# About the Author

Tunisia Williams is a middle school counselor who enjoys visiting zoos, aquariums, and wildlife safari parks. To relax, she goes boating on local lakes and rivers with her husband, Robert. They reside in Augusta, Georgia with their three dogs, Hope, Grace, and Coco.

CPSIA information can be obtained
at www.ICGtesting.com
Printed in the USA
BVHW021203120321
R11987600001B/R119876PG601863BVX00001B/1

9 781734 126174